Left and Right
Explores the human world

Mai Louise Falsig

Books on Demand

Mai Louise Falsig ~ Author

Left and Right
Explores the human world

Children's book

Drawings:
By **Anette Smed** ~ Copyright: 2014 Dorthe Klit

Drawings for deaf:
Center for deaf languae

ISBN 9788771457438

Publisher: Books on Demand GmbH, København, Danmark
Print: Books on Demand GmbH, Norderstedt, Tyskland

Proloque

This book is dedicated to the great group of people around the world for whom using hands have a far greater meaning than it has for others.

Not only do you use your hands to eat with, get dressed, drive, work, and more; but they are also artistic. I am not talking about painting, drawing or writing. No, they are used as languages. There are conjured beautiful language bouquets until that becomes a link between the deaf and / or deaf and dumb.

I definitely feel that it is one of the most beautiful forms of communication that exist.

It is also dedicated to our grandchildren: Gustav, Gunilla and Ayatsuki and grandchildren to come.

It is my hope that this book is not only a help in educating deaf and deaf-blind children. I also wish that it will provide children with normal hearing a little insight into the deaf world.

Finally, thanks to my daughter Tanja for ideas, inspiration and not giving up on me.

The hidden house

It was a small insignificant house. For the residents, it was just suitable; but for others, especially people, it was not to see.

It was sandwiched between two large human houses, and if one knew no better one could easily believe that this particular house was part of the facade.

Who lived in this house? There lived more families of hands. The house was on 16 floors, and there lived two families on each floor. On The ground floor there lived a pawnbroker in his small shop. It was such a place where you could pawn (deliver) some of your stuff. The pawnbroker then gave one some money in return. How much money you got depended on how much stuff you had pawned. If you later want your stuff back, you redeem just the pleged stuff. Now it's worth noting that he only took the pledge (meaning no mortgage which he had in his hand). You have to remember that he was a pawnbroker hand.

On the left of the ground floor, there was also a shop, a very distinguished glove maker. The owner was a refined hand called Miss Mitten. She was not married, and they called her "Mitten" because she, at first, could not do anything but gloves, when there were only a special pendant to your thumb arm. Now, however, she was very talented and made the finest clothes that no hand could wish for. Her lace gloves were admired by all, and they were every woman hand dream of a baldress.

On the 1st floor right there lived a couple of washing hands. They both worked all day long, in a restaurant where they washed plates, cups, glasses and cutlery all day long. All this work in the wash basin had made there skin so delicate and so wrinkled that they looked very old. And they were both even just 30 years old. At this age Mr. and Mrs. Dishwashing Hand had 3 kids, so there was plenty to do in their tiny flat. To the left, also on the 1st floor there lived a family of three. A single mother "Drawing Hand" with two younger children: Søs Drawing Hand and Nicolai Drawing Hand. Mother Drawing Hand was very good at painting, and she worked in the Royal Copenhagen factory where she only painted

6

mussel painted china (plates, cups, dishes and much more). She was at work, along with many others who were just like her. Because mussel painted porcelain was only quite right, if it was painted by hands.

On the 3rd floor on the right side there lived a workman's hand with his wife and a daughter. He was wrinkled from years of working in all kind of weather, where he had to work hard with no clothes on. He said that his work could not be done if he wear gloves. He was kind, and his daughter was a sweet little girl.

It was like this floor by floor one exciting family after another. The house was seething with life and many small hands. Because all families had children ~ well except the two shopkeepers at the ground floor.

High up in the attic lived a hand-clown. His wife was a tightrope walkerhand. They were blessed with two daughters, both of whom could perform many acrobatic numbers. All the residents in the entryway were very impressed with everything they could perform. Mr. Clown hand was a great success every time there was a child's hand, who celebrated his or her birthday.

Did I say all? But my goodness! You really must apologize. I have most definitely missed the 2nd floor above. Here lived some really nice hands. Mr. and Mrs. Hand. This is how they prefer to be called. Mr. Hand was a notary in the local bank. It was he who wrote the amounts in a book, every time other hands puts money in the bank. Which was a very trusted work; but Mr. Hand didn't brag with it. He was an ordinary friendly hand as his wife. Everyone in the entryway loved them dearly. The only way you could see that they had much money, was that their flat was the entire 2nd floor.

You would think that they were happy; but that wasn't so, they had no children. After some years, they had almost lost hope. Then they succeed. Mrs. Hand was pregnant and it was some very exciting months that they thought would never come to an end. Mr. Hand watched how Mrs Hand's belly grew and grew. She could no longer fit her gloves, and they had to go down to Miss. Mitten, to get her to sew new ones that fit. It was the clothes that Mrs. Hand had to wear while she waited for the baby to come into the world. You can almost call it maternity wear, thought Mr. Hand, and he was right. That's how the clothes was called that pregnant human women wore. Mother Hand's belly was finally so great that she could no longer move around inside the apartment. Finally it happend. The time had come.

The birth

The clock on the wall was quite slow. Tick tock it said, and father hand walked restlessly up and down the living room floor. Sometimes he could hear a soft moaning from inside the bedroom. It was mother hand, who was writhing in pain.

Now this birth must soon be over, he thought. It can not be right that it should last ages?

- Åååhhh! Mother hand howled. And shortly thereafter father hand heard a child crying. He stopped his ramble around the room, breathed a sigh of relief and wiped the sweat from his brow. Puh, ha! It had probably been a tough birth. Never in his life had he walked so much. And then around in his own room, he had almost become dizzy.

Now the child's crying was clearer, it was almost as if it was in stereo. The door opened, and the midwife send him a smile.

- You can get in now Mr Hand. The birth has successfully been completed. Come and see your 2 lovely boys. The midwife opened the door to the bedroom completely.

- 2 Boys!

Father hand almost shouted it out in the living room. He went with hesitant steps into the bedroom.

At the bedside was the doctor and he was dried out thoroughly. He nodded to father hand.

- Twins by my troth. More shapely boys are unthinkable.

9

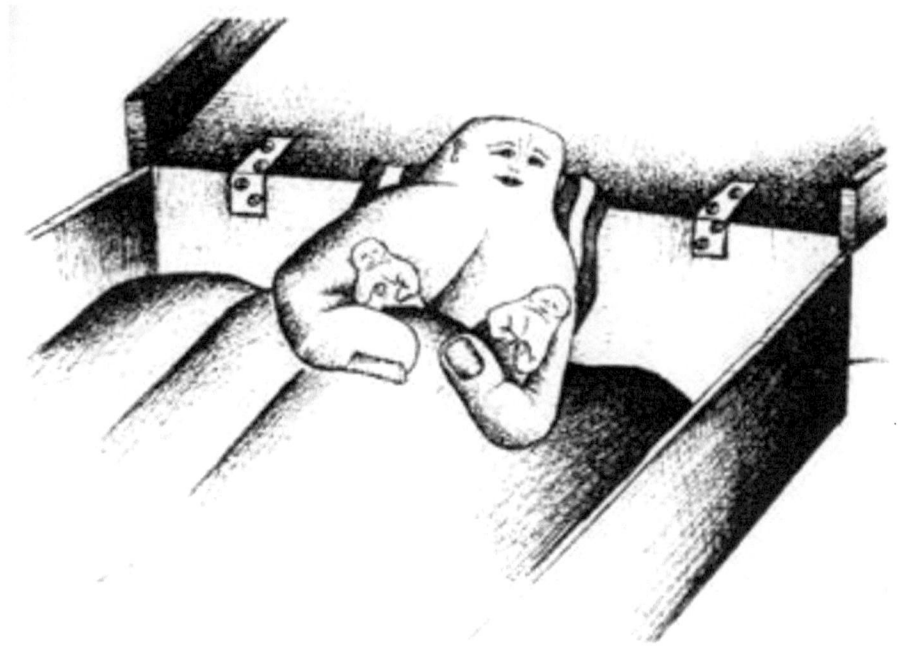

He began to take on his coat. It was freezing cold outside. Don't forget that it was the 24th of December.

- Merry Christmas, my love.

Father hand bent down over his wife and gave her a hug.

- And thank you for the Christmas presents. These are the best gifts that I have ever had.

He gave her a kiss on here forehead and rose again.

- And they are fine doctor?

Asked father Hand. He turned arround and looked at the doctor who was ready to go.

- Fine! They don't come better. Enjoy these 2 Christmas presents together with your wife. However, she needs to calm down it has been a long birth.

He said said goodbye and left the bedroom.

- Hold on! I will follow you out doctor!

Father hand went out in the hall said goodbye to both the doctor and the midwife. Then he closed and locked the frontdoor. Filled with pleasure and an internal pride he went back into the bedroom.

- Aren't they cute?

Mother hand smiled tired.

- They definitely are.

Father hand sat down beside her bed. Carefully he raised a corner of the duvet and then looked down at his boys.

- Have you seen that one is a left hand he is now to be called the awkward?

Mother hand looked worried.

- You know how other children can annoy.

- Nonsense! We live in enlighted times. There is nothing, which is called awkward. He is left, and his twin brother is a right hand, which is the way it should be.

He stood up again.

- Now you must rest a little. I'll go into the living room and enjoy this lovely Christmas eve. I'll see you a little later.

As he have said so. Father hand went into the living room sat down filled with joy and smiled a little inside. Just imagine, that they now were a family of four and among hundred of days on Christmas Eve itself. It is what I call a Christmas present.

This is how life began for **Left** and **Right**. They had been born. Although they were not wrapped up; however, as the best Christmas present any father and mother could wish for.

Getting older

Time passed, **Left** and **Right** grew up to become some small live wires, as such two healty boys have to be. Mother and Father Hand one afternoon looked at their twins, while they were playing on the floor in the living room.
- I can't understand that I was afraid of it would be a handicap for **Left** to be left-handed, said mother hand.
- They are, of course, some perfect boys both of them.
- Just my words! Father hand gave his wife a big hug, which means a handshake in the world of hands.

- I nearly forgot. You are also a left hand and there are nothing wrong with you.
Mother Hand hesitated
- You have never been teased as well?
She reciprocated her husband's handshake and sat down at the main dining table.
- No! Not as far as I can remember, and just consider how convenient it really is. We are never going to throw children's clothes away. We buy only a pair of gloves, and there are clothes for both of them. If our twins both were right hands, then we

should always throw one glove away. Father hand, looking relieved at the thought of all the money he saved on clothes.

The boys were playing, as told, in the living room; but they had a very large room completely for themselves.
- We have to go into our room, said **Right**. He would play something wild, and this wasn't allowed in the living room.
- That's alright.
Left stood up and went into the room. As soon as it was imposible to find any free floor space to play on, that wasn't crowded with gloves. There was thrown gloves all over the room.
- Why didn't you clear the room?
Mother hand stood in the doorway.
- I have said a thousand times that you should put it neatly together, and into the glove box! {Hands have cabinets like human beings; but as their clothes were gloves, they always called the cabinet a glove compartment.} Human beings wrongly thought that we are talking about a car's glove compartment, something that was in a car; but they are of course very different.

The gauntlet has been thrown

Left and **Right** began ostentatiously to clean up the room.
- She is somewhat angry! **Right** threw a bike-glove across the floor. It should have been put in the closet with trousers and T-

shirt in the same dress. It was now mid-September, and it was a month ago, that it had been good weather. The twins had to admit that they and their mom had misclculatet this autumn. They needed warm gloves.

- You mustn't throw the glove!
Left looked admonishing at his brother.
- Don't you remember when we saw the old movie with the four Musketeers at our TV? In the film an angry man throw a glove in front of another man, because he would fence with him to life or death. By throwing the gauntlet he challenge him explained their father then. I am not going to fence with you therefore stop throwing gloves.
- There are no one but us in the room, whom would I challenge? It's only if there are other hands in the room that I wouldn't.
Right answered his brother; but he still seemed a little scared. Just think if there were any, who would fence with him to life or death? He couldn't fence at all.

  Their mother closed the door giggling and walked into the living room where she sat in an armchair.

  As time went by, the twins became wiser and wiser. They have learned a great deal, because their father had purchased many books.They were called hand books. It was this kind of book, which hands read in. There were books about everything possible, and the twins lapped up all the words.

- Look! There is a bird. It has a ring around its leg. **Right** laughed and pointed at the drawing in the book.

- It is almost just like mum and dad. They have a ring on their legs as well. Maybee that enables us finds them again?

- It is not the same.

Left looked wondering at his brother. **Left** was a little old-wise and would very much like to reprimand his brother **Right**.

- Our mother and father have a ring on one leg, because they are married. It is called a marriage ring,... ... i think.

- I know!

Right closed the book with a snap.

- But I just think that it was fun that some birds also had a ring around its leg.

Work done by hands

They also learned that work done by hands were important. Without hands the world would soon be out of order, said their father. He believed that if there were no hands, the world would end up in chaos and a possible collapse. They knew that hands did most of it.

They wrote, were cooking, leafing through books, cutting trees, put bricks down in mortar in the wall.

Well, it is really the truth. Human beings could do nothing without hands.

They had also read something about various hand-work. Once again it was their dad, who told and explained. He meant simply that, to be a contractor, was the only correct training for any man. **Left** and **Right** agreed, but there was still something that plagued **Right**.

- I do not quite understand that craftmans ship should be so good. When father has a sore back of his hand and cannot be anywhere for pain, our mother says that a craftman works in his body. **Right** send a questioning look to his brother.

- It's true.

Left couldn't really understand, that craftmanship should be so good, when it caused so much pain. But as we all know, there was so much that one couldn't understand being just a child.

The reason that they have learned and read everything at home was that there really was no school only for hands. Their mother would not let them go so often out of the home. She said it was dangerous. You could be stepped on by people, bitten by dogs or run over by cars. The twins had seen the heavy traffic at times, when they had been with their parents in the city. It was dangerous but at the same time also very exciting.

They were, however, not always alone with their mother and father. They had many playmates, who visited them, and they also often paid them a visit. All friends lived with their parents in the same recovery. To see them wasn't dangerous at all. It was, as you should remember a narrow house, where only lived hands.

The twins like visiting their friends and a lot of fun as well. It would then be possible to play with any other toys, and playing with this was a lot of fun. It may well be that the people when they used the word hand-raise{enforce}, that it in their world mean secure that something is done correct{enforce the law}; but in hands world to enforce {hand-raice} was an elevator, in which one could raise hands from one floor to another. It tickled so funny in your stomach when you used it.

To Africa

One evening, while they were in the living room playing with their tiny toy cars, their mother and father where waching the television. They saw something about a red cross. It was not just only about the red cross, because they could both see and hear many people talk and entertain with songs and stand-up comedians. Suddenly they heard a woman's voice say;: "It is important that all of us give a hand to Africa." The twins stopped in the middle of their fun and looked scary at one another.

There would now be sent millions of hands to Africa. Perhaps some of their friends were sent too. They could hardly believe it. Then their mother suddently say.

- Shouldn't we help and give a hand as well?
Left and **Right** looked aghast at each other.

- I do not want to go to Africa, how can our mom get this crazy idea sending us to a foreign country? She doesn't want to have us anymore?
Right stood up and ran into his room. **Left** was right behind him, because he would neither go to Africa. They rushed into their room and closed the door.

- **Left**… **Right**! Shout their mother. She called on both of them. She would not just give one hand. No, they were both two be send away. They hide in a dark corner of the room. Their mom opened the door.

- Where are you? I've got hot chocolate.
Now she would, even lure them with chocolate. They didn't believe she was doing this.

- We don't want to go to Africa. You can donate any other hand.
Left said the last sentence very specific. Their mother at first looked at them being a big questin mark. Then she lit up in a huge grin.

- Africa… give a hand. Oh, some silly boys you are. When we say give a hand, it just means to help, to send some money. I did not intend to give you two away. The twins appeared eased out from their hiding. They gave their mother a handshake (crush) and ran to the coffee table. Now a cup of chokolade would do them well.

At bed time

Each evening, before they went to bed, it was time to take a bath. When you are a hand, you are taking a bath in a washbasin. It was not mounted at the same high at the wall as it was in the human world. Hands cannot take a bath unless their washbasin is standing on the floor. It was in fact their bathtub. Life was great. The twins always turned a little wild which meand that the whole bathroom floor sailed in water. It was not so bad being a hand.

That was one thing that was made specielt for hands. It is unneccesary to mention that they used hand soap, when they bathed. After the bath their mother lubricated them into hand lotion. Something which human beings calls handlotion; but it was however hand cream. Their mother lubricated them all over, and they smelled well, when the twins went to bed. They were sleeping together in a double bed. A hand luggage, which was opened.

In each half of the suitcase was a nice mattress with a warm duvet. Finally the bed also had the advantage that they could not fall out because of the high sides. After all they had a good and warm life.

They got all the food that they could eat. Their parents were loving and helpful. In addition, ampel clothes in a super quality. The glove cabinets were loaded with clothes. There were gloves made of fabric, gloves made of leather only to use when they were expected to troop up in their best outfit. And of course knitted gloves in a lot of colors their mother had knitted for them. And when it was hot in the summer they went with cycling gloves, for they had short legs. Not only knitted their mother diligently. So much fun, as she kept choosing-pin with her thumb- and litle finger arms. Their father had to help. For, as you know, it is neccesary whit two pair of hands, if you are going to knit. Their clothes were very expensive, their mother told them, due to the fact that she used only pure wool. {in danih called clean wool}

Right thought that it was obvious. Who would be very keen on having gloves knitted in dirty wool? But he fully understood that the wool was expensive. When the yarn factories had washed it for their mother, they would have to earn money for their work. She also stitched much of the family's clothing herself.

20

The twins knew no better than to play in the living room, where their father happy smoked his pibe, and the sound of the old seewingmachine's wheel cheerfully spinning.

Their dad knew a store down on the corner, where he could get the finest towels it was the fabric their mom used, when she made clothes to all of them. He bought and bought. But now their mom had said that it had to stop. She had fabric for year's way ahead.

Bored
Exploring the city

Years passed by, and the twins were now 11 years old. They were looking forward to their confirmation.

In the world of hands the baptism was ratified, when they were 12 years old. They had learned, from their nieces and nephews, that one get many gifts from near and far. It was early in the morning. Their dad was at work, and mom was in the kitchen baking buns. The twins were a little bored. They knew every inch of the flat and had not been out for a long time, because it was December, and the cold and the snow had put its clammy hand over the city.

Their dad had tried to explain the meaning of a clammy hand to them. But they had not really grasped that a hand could be clammy. **Left** was convinced that it had to be something with cool, when it now was so freezing cold.

The twins walked out in the hand corridor {håndgangen in Danish} Human beings say that of course it could mean to be faithful; but among hands it simply mean the entrance hall. They looked at the row of thimble which stood at parade. Thimbles were hands shoes. Suddenly **Left** got an idea.

- **Right** Why don't we take our coats on and take a walk in the street. Our mom discovers nothing. We are back home again in no time?

He pulled his brother **Right** in the thumb.

- I really don't know.

Right wasn't keen on walking in the street without permission from their mother. They had never been alone on the street before.

- It is dangerous!

He tried to curb his brother's crazy idea.

- Nonsense, we will take care. Wouldn't it be exciting? **Left** was now very keen, and it was not long before than he had persuaded his brother to a small excursion. An adventure, as he called it.

Out in the street

They took on their warmest knitted gloves, a woolly hat and thimbles. **Left** opened the door slowly. There was nobody in the stairwell. The door creaked a little and **Left** stopped horrified.

- What did I say? Mom will hear s any minute!

Right wriggled back into the entrance hall.

- Come on! She heard nothing, hury up…please.

Left withdrew **Right** out in the stairwell and carefully closed the door. **Left looked** down the stairwell to see if there were any other hands, while **Right** pressed the button to hand-raiser {the elevator}. It seems like several hours before than the hand-raiser stopped on their floor, and the door opened.

- It is here now, come on! **Right** was yelling at his brother.

- Shyyyyss! **Left** rushed over and shushed on **Right**.

- Don't shout so loud! What if anybody hear us?

They went into the hand-raiser, pressed the button for the street and drove down tight to break-point.

When they were down. They quickly ran to the front door and opened it.

They opened it even very quiet. Not only were they a little bit afraid; but the door was also very heavy. So heavy that they almost didn't get it up. When they finally got out on the street the sight overwhelmed them. The snow was covering everything like a thick white blanket. Nearly too thick for the twins and went up in the middle of their three finger legs. Bearing in mind that they were not very high, that even a little snow was a lot to them. Many human beings went down the sidewalk, and the twins pressed close against the wall. Cars drove quickly out on the street. It was a terriblel racket and hustle.

- We have to to go up again? We have now been right down on the street.

Right was not much for this adventure.

- No! We just move close to the house wall. The human beings do not walk that close to the walls, so there is nothing to be afraid of. **Left** began trudging along the sidewalk in the high snow, and **Right** followed him hesitant. When they had gone a few minutes **Right** stopped.

- **Left**!...Look!

Right pointed eagerly up at all the people.

- Theywalk around with hands like us. At the end of all their arms. Do you see it? I want to be carried as well.

- That's impossible, It is fun to go here in the snow too. **Left** looked inquisitively at a man, who in the same moment pasted by. He had hands as well, and he did care for them. **Left** was able to see that they had clothes (gloves) on. He looked at several people, and the had also hands. Amazing, it had their mother and father never told them. Here they thought that there were not a great many hands throughout the world. Perhaps only those in their own recovery. And now he discover that it teemed with hands on all people.

   A little further down the sidewalk was an older woman walking. She had both arms inserted into a sleeve made of fur, which were based on her stomach.

- She has no hands.

Right shouted amazed.

- She has no hands…why not?

Left was just as surprised, as his brother, and he watched the woman for a long period.

- I know it! You can see that she has a handbag. Her hands are guaranteed in her bag.

- Are you serious?

Right was doubtfull.

- Yep! That is why it is called a handbag. Perhaps she has no gloves to put on her hands. That is why she has placed them into the bag.

They were very impressed that people did so well with respect to their hands. Not to forget, that on top of that, they carried them around in a bag. The old woman passed by them at the sidewalk, in the same moment, and snow from her shoes soles, sprayed over the twins. The twins knocked to the ground and rolled around in the snow. They laughed and have a great fun.

- It is lots of fun.

Right got up and looked at his brother.

- You look like a snow hand, he laughed.

Left throw a snowball after him and laughed just as loud as **Right**.

The disabled

They brushed both the snow of their gloves and continued along the pavement. When they had walked only a few meters, they were looking at a man in a wheelchair. It was really amazing. He used hands in order to move. He was not at all like the other people they have seen.
-Why doesn't he walk? Do you think that his legs are tired?

Right could not help but look at the man who stopped at a crosswalk and waited for the green light.
- I do not know, perhaps he has no legs.

Left was impressed by, a human being, who could only walk {move around} because some hands helped him. It was true, what their father had said. Hands are involved in many things. Slowly they went closer and to their amazement, he had just Drivers Gloves on his hands.
- Look! He has short trousers on his hands! Even its very cold.
Now **Left** was really mad. How could a human being wear driver gloves on his hands, when it was minus 10 degrees Celsius?
- They are probably not freezing, when they are going to do so much work.
That was Right's opinion and he almost felt sorry for the hands, which should work this hard. Just because a person did not use his legs.

In the same moment a carpet over the man's legs slipped aside, when he began to move his wheelchair out in the crosswalk. The twins noticed that he lacked both legs. That was why two hands had to help him.

- This kind of work I would very much like to have, when I am an adult.

Right fell into a reverie.

- I was unable to do such a job, and in short gloves as well.

Left shook intended on the head.

- If I would be something; it was someone, who was talking all the time.

- You know that there are people who Can't hear or speak, and use their hands in order to talk!

Left believed that this had to be a good and important work. He had read about it, in one of their manuals at home, and he couldn't find any-thing more exciting than to be the one who made sure that deaf people were able to talk together. Once, he had been in a museum together with his father, he had seen two girls standing talking with each other, but only with their hands. It's fun allright; but it was also hard work. Becase he only saw, that their hands all the time did a lot of fun characters and shapes. The Girls said nothng, they only used their hands. At first he found it strange, but the fact that his father had told him, why they spoke together like this, he had been very concerned about it. He had at home tried to make language characters; but he soon realized that it was necessary to sit at the end of an arm to get it just right.

- Yes, almost as with boxers.

Right was immediately fire and flame.

- You know boxers, as we have seen at home on the television. Dad says that they let their fists do the talking. They talk with their hands too.

Right began boxing on his brother.

- It is not the same... When deaf people do so, then it is to talk together. When it is boxer's handss, it is in order to win a boxing match.

Left said the last words with a very admonishing tone. He thought that he was smarter than his brother.

- It is not the same as like saying something. Boxing hands wear also so much clothes, that we cannot even see what they have to say in the great boxing gloves ... Basta!

Left moved on.

The Pharmacy

A little further down the street they saw a large sign that read: "Pharmacy". It looks like a popular shop, because many people were going out and in through the door.

- Let's see what is happening inside the shop? **Right** began to run.

- Okay! **Right** please wait!

Left ran after him, and they reached toward the door at the same time. The next time the door went up they got rushed in with a very large lady. She had a brown coat and the edge of her flower-rich dress hanging beneath her coat.

- Look! She has eel in her tights.

Left pushed to his brother.

Right seems it was very crazy to carry eels around. He looked forward with eager anticipation to the woman's tights; but he could not see any eel. Perhaps it was possible because she had fishnet tights on, and he had read that you use nets to catch eels. Once again he studied her tights; but he could still not see any creeping eels.

- There are no eels!

He looked disappointed at his brother.

- Of course there are eels, said **Left**.

- Naturaly they are not really live eel; but when her pantyhose are located in folder, it is said that she has eel in her stockings. Our mom once told me.

Right was really disappointed. He had been looking forward to see some eels crawling around. He had never seen a live eel, and now it was all just nonsense.

He looked around in the shop and suddenly froze. He pulled gently at his brother and pointed scared up at a sign over some shelves. "Hand-purchase" in big black letters. He could not see more, as the woman in the brown coat blocked for the rest of the sign. Hand-purchase {Prescription}.

Right was now almost in shock.

- Have you seen the sign **Left**? Hand-Purchase! It is possible to buy hands. I did not know. Do

29

you think, that we are bought here? He was about to cry. Imagine, their mom and dad had just bought them down at the pharmacy. Now the tears began running down his cheeks.

Left said comforting.

- I do not know. No they haven't. Mother has even told me about how we were born. It was a doctor and a midwife, who came with us.

- Have they bought us here?

Right hiccoughed.

- Now I know neither in nor out of the whole matter.

- No, no!

Left almost cried.

- They helped mother to give birth to us, back home in mother and father's bedroom.

Right dried the tears away and was very glad. He had been afraid that they were just purchased here at the pharmacy. Yet he felt not really safe and asked his brother, if he don't mind leaving the pharmacy and move out on the streets again. Imagine if there was someone, who wants to buy them, and then they would never return home to their mother and father. They went toward the door and waited until it was opened by a human being. They went out on the stairs in hurry and then crawling down the high steps. It was almost life threatening for it was high. However, it was easier than they had beleived. They had been forced to stand on top of each other to achieve. And they had almost been stepped on by several human beings while they climbed. Finally, they were down leaving the pharmacy quickly behind. The woman with eels in her pantyhose walked past them with a firm step and **Right** was still not sure whether she saw an eel up under her coat.

At the drugstore.

They had become thirsty, and searched for something to drink. They had heard something about a Hand Beer. It was their dad's favorite beer, and he enjoyed one or two every Saturday night, A Hand-Beer is definitely something that hands could drink.

Suddenly they caught sight of a grocery store. Super! They knew both that it was in such a store one could buy something to drink.

However, after the incident at the pharmacy they were somewhat scared. The letters "Grocery store" were painted on a large sign above the door. "Buy-man" {the Danish name for a "Grocery store"}.

Right was very worried..

- Do you think that they are selling or buying men?...I mean, when you can purchase hands at the pharmacy?... The world, outside our home, is a strange size.

Left shrugged.

- I don't think so; but you never know. I'm not 100% sure...Do you really think, that one can buy men too? ... Where are the human beings then buying and selling women?

Left was confused and uncertain. He suddenly felt stupid and far from a wise young hand. All this debate regarding buying and selling Hands and or people. He straightened his hand back.

- No, It is definitely in this store, that we can get a drink.

They approached the door and looked up at the handle. They also had handles in the doors at home; but they could be reached.

Left climbed up on top of the **Right**. But no matter how much he stretched, he could not reach. At that moment the door was opened from within, and they fell on a woman's shoes. They rolled around in the dust on the floor and sat dazed up.

They climbed quickly to safety along one wall just inside the door. When they had recovered a little, they stood up and walked over to the grocery counter.

- Oh, my, how the disk is high!

Left looked for a human being.

- How do we get in contact with the merchant when we hardly are able to see him due to the tall disc?

This meant at least, that it was no use standing on top of each other.

Right kicked the disk to point out that they were there; but inothing happened. No one could hear them. They hammered both on the front of the disk; but it made little difference.

- Hello! **Left** cried.

He had been angry, as he believed they were ignored.

A deep voice echoed in the higher altitudes:

- Ups…Sorry!

In the same second a pencil dropped down on the floor next to them. It was a purely luck that they were not affected. It had fallen down from the grocery disk. The twins bowed their neck as much as possible and saw the voice's owner. They stared into a head full of hair all over. It was the merchant. He looked at them with his nice eyes.

Left was shocked.

- Hey…Be carefull!

- Oh! What do we have here?

The merchant watched them with great interest. He looked almost as if he had never seen a pair of hands before; but it couldn't be true. The twins noticed that he even had hands at the end of his arms, as all the other people they had seen.

- We would like one Hand Beer…please.

Left remembered that the bottle was far too big for one child hand.

- Yes, this I believe. Do you have any hand-ears? {Human beings said usually pennies}.

The merchant chuckled cheerfully of his own joke.

- Yes, of course we have. Otherwise we could not hear anything.

Left thought that it was a strange question.

- I mean money.

The merchant has stopped laughing and then again looked down on them.

Right and **Left** looked at each other.

Money! They never thought about money. The twins had read about it in one of their dad's many books; but they had not really understood why they had to spend money. They had never even had any money. At home, they had everything they needed. Perhaps their mum and dad had some money.

- No, we have no money.

Right were embarrassed that they penniless had tried to buy a Hand Beer.

- And you will still have a hand beer. It is not meant for small sizes like you. You should rather have a soda or an orange Juice…What are you really? You're hands! How do you drink?

The merchant stopped his flow of speech and wiped his forehead with a cloth.

- By our mouth!

Left was sick and tired of being looked at like this. Everybody believes that we're a couple of strange animals that had escaped from the zoo. Why did it take him aged to discover, that they were Hands?

- Yes, of course through the mouth. Why didn't I immediately figure that out?

The merchant was ready to burst.

- What are you doing in this part of the city on your own…hand?

He chuckled again by his own joke.

- We're just out to have a look around.

Right moved closer to his brother.

- Can't you see that we're just two hands that are thirsty?

The merchant had never seen anything like it in all the many years that he had lived, and now he was soon 60 years old. Was he dreaming, or was he awake. He called on Michael, who was his assistant in the grocery store.

- Michael!

The merchant's voice was shrill.

- MICHAEL!

Just then Michael was lumbering into the store.

- Now what? What are you yelling for?

Michael stuck one finger into his ear and rotated it around, as if he would provide more room for the sound. So he better could hear when the shopkeeper shouted.

- Try to look down on the floor in front of the counter. The merchant was looking expectantly at him. Michael thought it was very strange that he should look down on the floor but did it anyway to please the merchant. He was almost in shock, down in front of him stood a left and a right hand wearing gloves, woolly hat and thimble. He was speechless.

- Tell me something Mike.

The merchant nudged him.

- What do you think of it? Do you also see a pair of hands?

Michael could nothing but nod.

Yes! At least he didn't dream, or both he and Michael were dreaming.

The merchant decided not to be affected.

- This is Michael, my sidekick…my assistant. Do you want a soda?

The merchant looked down on **Left** and **Right**.

- Yes, thank you. **Left** was ever so thirsty.

- Lissen… **Left**! The merchant said to me that his assistant was a hand hoses. Do you think that he, like the pharmacist hoses hands over the counter?

Right was certainly not comfortable with the situation.

- Never in a million years. Forget the pharmacy. Let's enjoy this soda.

Left walked towards the two small cups with orange juice, which the merchant had put on the floor in front of them. In each cup there was a tiny straw so they could get it into their mouth. They took their hats of and sucked, so it was a pleasure, and soon the cups were empty. Aaaahhh! How it helped. **Left** and **Right** again took their bobble hats on. With a bye, bye they walked towards the door. **Left** looked at the merchant:

- Please open the door we cannot reach up to the handle?
- Yes, of course. The merchant opened the door and then looked bemused after the two tiny hands. Now he had something to tell Anna. She was his wife, and she didn't bother assist in the store. It was boring. There was never anything exciting, she said.

Michael, who again had his voice back shouted:
- Goodbye!

The twins turned around on the sidewalk
- Goodbye, they said in unison turned and walked contentedly further down the street.

The merchant closed the door locked it and put the sign that read, "Gone for dinner" in the door. Now he really needed a break.

   Right did not say much, he wondered over the human world, where you could buy both a man and a hand. He had even now seen one that reached hands across the counter, a real sidekick. It was good that he wasn't so often out in the human world.

The Airport

The ride

After walking for a while, they decided to get back to their mother and father. **Left** was sure that he knew the way. For he had noticed all the houses which they had passed.

- Woof! Woof! Grrrrrr! A large dog was standing less than a meter from them. The dog barked loudly and showed its teeth. They had not discovered it. They were so aborbed in their own thoughts. Terrified they turned away from the dog and the road.

- Woof! The dog walked slowly closer, and saliva was dripping from the corners of the mouth and teeth onto the pavement. Now the twins were really scared. They had now reached the far curb, before the road.

- What do we do?

Cried **Right**? He was very scared.

- It is going to eats us we never see our mom and dad anymore. Who will tell them that we have been eaten by a dog?

Tears rolled down the little hand.

    They had, in the midst of their big nightmare not discovered that they were right out in front of a bus stop.

One of these new low-floor buses stopped the very moment behind the twins. A low-floor bus was made so you could drive right into the bus with a wheelchair or a pram.

Left and **Right** took another step back to get away from the dog fell over the small crack between the bus and the curb and tumbled into the bus. They rolled under a seat to get to safety for the many people who swarmed into the bus. The door closed, and passengers heard a voice in the speaker say:

- Next stop domestic terminal at the airport!

- What the hell!

Left looked at his brother.

- We are now on our way to the airport isn't where all the planes are?

Right nodded. Their dad had, as recently as yesterday, told them a lot about airplanes and airports.

- I'm not going to the airport, I want to go home!

Right was sorry over the fact that he had been lured along on this trip.

- Do not worry. We'll get home. When we have seen the airport and all the planes, then we'll go home to mom and dad.

Left comforted soothing his brother.

The bus lurched through the city, and the twins had to stick with hoops underneath the seat not to scroll up and down the bus's floor. They thought it lasted an eternity; however the people were silent.

People - they never speak to each other. **Right** could not help but wonder if the people on the bus were sad. They were maybe reluctantly going to the airport since they were so silent. Surely no one had forced them? He could now pretty well understand that they did not say anything. He did not even want to talk because it certainly was not with his good will that he was on his way to the airport. **Left** on the other hand looked curious around the bus.

He was excited to see all the planes, and he was very relieved that they had escaped the teeth of the ferocious dog.

After a 20 minutes drive the bus stopped.

- Domestic Terminal! The sound came from a speaker and more people got off the bus; but there were also many who stood on. Before the twins could get off the bus, it left the bus stop and was running on. It did not run very far before than the bus stopped again.

- The international terminal! The speaker crackled. Meanwhile, the twins had climbed all the way to the door. Just as human feet did.

The International airport

When they were safe, they looked baffled in the air and out to the sides. Never, they had seen such a large building before.

Not even at home in their street in the city, had they seen such a huge house.

- Do you think that the aircrafts are inside the house, since it is so large, asked **Right**? **Left** thought as it creaked. He believed that he had seen that the aircrafts stood outside the houses.
- I don't think so, he replied; but he was not really sure regarding this matter.
A plane took off in the same second, and it made a lot of noise. The twins watched with tense while the plane lifted its big shiny body up against the clouds.
- It is going to get up and lie on the clouds, said **Right**.
- It can take a brake and rest there while the cloud flies away with the aeroplane inside the cloud.

- A flying cloud, he exclaimed cheerfully. - A flying cloud! As he was talking he danced around his brother **Left**.

Left thought it made sense, all this about the cloud; but on the other hand they did not know much about flying.

They approached the large glassdoors, while they made sure not to get in the way of people's feet.

Imagine being walked to death just before you would see an airport. As they approached the front door, it opened up suddenly, without anyone had touched it.

- These doors should have been everywhere, said **Left** excited.

- Hands could also get in without help. What they did not know was, that there was mounted a sensor which Is able to sense when a human being approach the door. It is set to open the door immediately at the time a person is approachhing. Such a sensor could not spot a pair of hands.

They went into the big arrival and departure hall. Shut the fuck up it's great. There were so high ceilings the twins had to lie down to see all the way up. There were lots of shops, a throng of people of all colors. The twins looked around in amazement.

They had never seen a black, or for that matter a brown man before.

- He's probably sunburned, **Right** tried to find an explanation when a man black man at that moment went past them.

- I have never been so brown. I've always been really out in the sun a lot during the summer. **Right** was quite envious. Now, **Left** has happened to read about people with different skin colos, and he hissed quietly on his brother.

- Not so loud. It may be that someone will hear us. It is not a tan. There are people in other countries, who many years ago developed this color, because it was better for them in their own country, where it is hotter than with us. **Right** was impressed. However, it was incredible that his brother knew that much. They went to the floor against all the many barriers, where there was a woman in every desk. They were smiling and spoke to many people. In front of each desk there was a long queue. It took an eternity before the twins reached over to the other side. We should remember that they did not go with such large steps, and they should also avoid people's feet.

At one of the counters was a very sweet red-haired woman. She smiled and said to the female passenger who stood in front of the counter.

- You are only allowed to have the bag, which is in your hand into the plane as hand luggage suitcase. The remaining suitcases have to go into the plane's luggage compartment. **Left** and **Right** looked dismayed at each other. Hand-luggage! It was perhaps true, the words that were painted on the sign inside the pharmacy. Hand-luggage. She had guaranteed purchased a lot of hands. Danish hands! And now this red-haired woman was going to fly away with them.

- It is terrible, said **Left**. He withdrew his brother a little away from the desk.

- Now she is taking a lot of hands far from Denmark. Maybe it's against their will. They do not want to fly away!
- We'll have to save them!
Right interrupted his broyher.
- Come on let's follow the woman. As decided. They ran after her, but the twins could not go as quickly as she could. Thankfully she sat down at a Café not far away from where they had stopped and she placed her handbag on the floor next to the chair. They snuck quiet all the way to the bag. It was closed with something weird sik sak something with a flat stick at one end.
- Damn **Left** had with difficulty been lifted up on top of the bag with a lot of help from **Right**, and God help me if the bag was closed. The hands were locked up. He could not know that it was just a zipper, one like he had never seen before in his short life.
- It is closed!
Left bent carefully over the edge and whispered down to his brother. The woman in the same moment bent down With the finger on her left hand she took hold of the pin to the zipper.
Left was so frightened that he rolled off the edge of the bag.
Fortunately he got hold of the handle and slipped down on the floor to his brother **Right**.
- Wow! It was close. **Left** was trembling all over.
- Look! She didn't close her bag again. I'll have to go up there!
Once again, he was standing on top of **Right** and came with some difficulty up upon the bag again. He climbed slowly to the edge of the open zipper and then into the bag. No hands! There was

only a lot of things, a woman always have in her bag. **Left** had to admit, that the handbag was crowed. Any woman could survive on a desert island whit this bag.

The hands must be stored inside, thought **Left**. He dived into her belonging in the bag righ. **Right** followed anxious every second the scenery from the floor. **Left** searched every corner; but he could find no hands. When he had been diving in the contens of the bag, the woman in the same¨moment rose and picked the bag up from the floor.

- Oh! No! **Right** cried out loud, and, at the same time he ran after the woman. Now, his brother **Left** was to be transported out of the country along with all the other hands.. He didn't know that **Left** had found no hands. The whole situation was not looking so well from **Left's** point of view **Left** was down in her bag; but the woman fluctuated so much with the bag that **Left** was about to be seasick. Fortunately she was going to buy some sweets and magasines for the flight. She put her bag down on the floor in the duty free shop. **Left** crawled stumble up, then slipped down the handle landed on the floor and sank dizzy on his back next to his brother.

- Have you been drinking, asked **Right**.

- Was there something in her bag that you drank of **Left**? You are drunk!

Right laughed and withdrew his brother to safety.

- You are hand-drunk. Just like mum and dad on New Year's Eve. Hand-drunk is said about hands of course, if they drank too much wine, schnapps or too many beers.

- I am not drunk, I only feel dizzy, because the woman swung her bag all the time.

Left snapped at his brother.

- There were no hands?
Right pulled curious his brother.
- No. there was no hands. The whole matter regarding hand-luggage was totally wrong - fortunately.
Left was now better so he went from lying to sittig position.
- The red-haired woman at the desk thought perhaps that she had her bag full. They were still a little angry at the woman and stared evil as she walked over to the stairs on the other side of the hall. She could have had a bag filled with hands. It had been hard on them, and they sat down a bit just outside the duty free shop.

The Escalator

- I'm hungry. **Right** looked longingly toward the cafeteria.
- I would like a hand food. Hand sandwiches, it was that they ate at home with their mother and father.
Left replied resignedly.
- You can not get any ... do you understand? He was really hungry
- We have no ... Was it money, the merchant said?
They had to patiently wait until they again were at home. Although their small hands rumbled with hunger. They had not eaten since this morning, and now the time was soon 2PM.
- Let us forget that we are hungry.
Left encouraged his brother.

- Come on, we have to see everything here. Then we will go home.
- Promise?

Right was soon as indifferent to airport, aircraft and the whole excursion as anyone could be. He would like to return home and get something to eat. His finger feets were aching due to the many hours in a thimble. He was tired of it all. They looked cross the hall and suddenly the eye discovered a staircase which was running on its own. A rolling staircase named so by the people. They cheered up at the sight. Curious, as such, a couple of kids of course are, they could not hold back. They hurried over to the other side and approached cautiously this marvel of a staircase.

- Oh, my!

Right cried wildly.

- Such a staircase should everyone possess. Then we would not stand on top of each other and painstakingly pull us up each step. The staircase is running by itself **Left** nodded he was impressed too. They ran into a step and drove with the stairs up to First Floor. They held out close to one of the sides in order not to be crushed under the heel of a human being's shoe as the people definitely had to use the stair.

- People are somehow crazy,

Left didn't understand them.

- Why go when you can be transported all the way up?

Right had for a long time believed that people were weird so he didn't bother to comment what his brother said.

When the step reached the 1st floor they jumped for their life out on the floor to avoid being crushed. They looked along the long walk. Wow! It was long.

Check - in

At the other end there was an odd port in which the people went through. Sometimes the port made a lot of noise. The twins laughed. They had never seen a port like this before. Next to the port was a big machine, where people put their handbags and bags on a broad band. The band was running and the luggage disappeared into the machine.

- Do you think the machine eat the bags? **Right** wants to know.. Perhaps it was just as hungry, as he was.

- I do not know.

Left had never seen such a machine before, so he had no idea in or out of the matter.

They walked and they walked. They had never walked in so long a gangway even a smooth one. It was so smooth that they the whole time with their tiny finger legs slipping out to the sides. It was almost before, that their little legs could not bear them a step further

When they came up to the machine, the twins discovered the fact that it was possible to see the contents of the bags, which were in possession of he machine's "stomach".

- Its amazing!

Right was surprised.

- It is just like the hospital. When you are x-rayed the doctor is able to see if you are sick inside.

Left nodded and was fully in agreement with his brother.

- It is guaranteed in order to see if some bags are sick inside. You are probably not allowed to take a sick bags in the plane to fly to other countries!

Left thought that this must be the explanation. There was surely no country, which would receive sick bags. One bag passes after the other. They turned and saw a uniformed man standing with a strange little thing. It was a hand that held it. As did all his work. The uniformed man led just his arm around the traveler, and then led his hand search all around the person with the scanner. They saw a young man in a furry coat be searched with the scanner.

- I think it's a vacuum cleaner. **Left was sure**.

- The door reveals if you have lint on the clothing. You just dust them off. Incredibly smart?

Right had no better explanation. It made sense that you weren't allowed to have lint on the plane. Now it was a woman who was vacuumed. **Right** was a little offended that people did not leave their lint at home, if so the uniformed man didn't have to work so hard.

The twins had never been in an airport before. They could not have a clue about why you had to go through such a port. People who are allowed to fly, is forced to go through the gate and their bags to be examined, because you will not have knives, explosives or guns in the aeroplane. It should be safe to fly for all the peoples of the world.

Right did notice that all people were allowed to pass inspection. No matter if they were white, brown or black.

- It is strange that the bags and clothes are studied so much when it does not matter what color people are. **Right** almost growled to himself.

- It might be different with people.

Left could not really give a good explanation.

Who knows if people did not also have problems with their skin color in some countries? It would not surprise him. Their father had said that when something seemed to be "black" {gloomy}, it was not very good. He had, at the airport, seen many people who were "black" and they were okay. Their father had probably remembered wrong when he told them.

They began the long hike back down the long hallway. They could easily have sneaked past the gate and X-ray machine; but they did not exactly feel like flying. Why should they fly to another country?

They were the happiest with their mother and father. And what if other countries do not have hands? Who should they talk and play with? They walked and walked. They had completely given up hope when they finally came to an escalator that ran down. They raced to a step and went down again in the departure hall. **Right** stood right out on the edge of the step. There were such grooves, which he could balance on his thimble. When they were down **Left** stepped out on the floor.

Right made a hand (s)-turn and cheered happy. People call a hand (s) turn anything they can do so easily and quickly; but in the hands world meant a hand (s) turn just to turn a somersault. **Right** had hit a somersault on the floor. He got up and struck his thumb and little finger arm out to the sides.

- I'm flying! I fly, he cried.
- Look **Left**! Now I take off!

His brother ran over and pushed him hard, so hard that **Right** rushed to the side with a bang and rolled several times on the floor.

Right was about to scold his brother, when he saw a stiletto from a woman's shoes set down to the floor just a few inches from his body.

- Pyy!

Sighed **Left**

- It was close.

Little by little the first shock was gone and **Right** came on the feet.

He ran over to his brother and gave him a big hand pressure (hug).

- Thank you!

He stutters.

- You saved my life.

Now they wanna go home. There was too dangerous in the human world.

M & M's

They ran across the hall wide floor, reached safety over on the other side, where all the shops were. Slowly they walked along the glass facades, passed the kiosk and had to stand still. Otherwise they would run into the feet of a little boy. He stood with his mother and father and was about to eat merrily from a bag of M & M's.

- Hurry up and finish the bag. His mother was sighing.
- We have to go now. Otherwise we do not catch the plane. You can at least stop the bag in your pocket.
- No I do not, the boy replied curtly.
- Then put it down! His mother was now very angry.
  - Set it! We have candy. for the flight.

The boy put the bag down along the glass right next to the twins.

- Mother look two hands! The boy pulled eagerly his mother's coat.
- You can wash your hands in the plane, come on!

His mother pulled him away. She had not heard what he actually said. He followed rebellious his mother, while he curiously followed the twins with his eyes.

When they could not see him any more, they approached the bag. **Left** carefully took one M & M up between his finger arms.

- It's red! **Left** investigated further. He put it very gently in his mouth.

- It tastes good! Take one **Right**!
He could hardly speak, so great was the
lozenge.
- You are talking very funny!
Right laughed.
- I can not understand you. It's like
the "Silence sweets," which we get
at home with mom and dad. **Right**
also took one in his mouth,
a blue one, and they sucked merrily in unison. There were only
two pieces left in the bag, and they decided to eat them before
they left the airport.

When they were finished, they were not so hungry more. A few
M & M's saturates incredibly, when you're only a small hand.
They left the departure hall and went to the bus stop. Luckily,
there was only this one stop otherwise they might not take the
right bus into town. They could not see what was written on the
sign; but the twind decided certain that it was "City Centrum".

The journey Home

They waited, and they waited. Finally the big blue-gray bus
arrived. It looked almost like a monster, where the lights were
huge shiny eyes. With screeching brakes it stopped right in front
of the twins. Wisely they had gone a little to the side and waited
until there were no more people who went into the bus, before
they jumped onto the floor. Again they sat down under a seat wise
by experience.
- We'll have to be at the door, said **Left**.

- Otherwise we would not know when to get off the bus.

Right agreed. The twins huddled against a pole, which was right next to the door and looked tense out on all the houses, and the people who cycled. The twins had never heard of or seen a bike before except in their books. So it was quite an experience.

After nearly a half hour drive, **Right** saw the grocery store.
- It's here! There's the grocery store! This is where we need to get off the bus!

Right was happy to see the home environment.

Luckily there was a woman who had to get off the bus just this place. How could they ever be able to say to the bus driver that he should stop when they had to leave the bus and go home to their mother and father?

The woman went out, and the twins jumped after her. There was damned well over the edge; but they did jumps with ease. **Right** looked anxiously to both sides.
- What are you looking for? **Left** had already gone over to the house wall.
- I am looking for the big vicious dog.

Right was not quite sure if it really was gone. - There is no dog. Come on!

Left hurried to his brother. **Right** quickly ran after the **Left**, which had started to walk down the street toward the pharmacy.

They walked past the courthouse, where two police officers were on their way, and they had a man between them. He had his hands on his back, and when they disappeared up the stairs, the twins could clearly see a pair of handcuffs on the man's hands.

- A strange contraption that they put around the man's hands, and in iron!

Right was sorry on behalf of all hands.

- He has his hands behind his back. So he can not really keep an eye on them, believed **Left**.

- It's probably because the hands are not to disappear, he has them assembled in handcuffs!

Yes, he was sure of himself.

Right didn't care. He certainly would not like to go with a collar of iron around his neck.

- Can't he go by himself, since the police support him?

Right speculated on the fact that police officers almost dragged him up the stairs.

- He can probably not. Perhaps that is why he should be admitted to a hospital.

Left had heard of hospitals where you cured people. It was still strange that the man walked between two doctors when he was in the hospital.

Right said:

- Of course, it is the hospital.

The twins could not know that the man was a robber. He had stolen some money in a bank, and he was going into court and accused before a judge, then to be put in jail.

Left ran on.

Hold it! I would almost want a hand brake in you. You run so fast. I can not keep up!

Right cried breathless.

Left slowed down as he immediately was straight out of a sporting goods store. There were handballs in the window. He looked thrilled. Such handball he would like to own. Their father had said: "If they absolutely had to have a handball, he would make one for them." **Left** could see that it was too big. Yes, it was almost more than he. So maybe they should let their father make one.

Right next to the sports shop was a small store. A sign in the window, that hung over some wine bottles. There stood hand-picked specifically for you. They both agreed that it was odd. Just over some wine bottles. They only knew the word hand-picked from their mother.

She went every summer into a woman hand that plucked all the hairs of her finger legs. It did not look so pretty with all that hair, she said. For people could handpicked both mean that something was picked by hand; but it could also mean that they were specifically designated to one or some other work. They realized that they had to be out among the people, so they had to learn all the words and their meaning again. **Right** pushed to his brother even very rough.
- We must move on, I'm cold. I want to go home!
- Then don't push. It hurts. You are hand evil. **Left** was angry at his brother. He would also like to go home, his brother did not have to push. Finally they came to the pharmacy, now they were soon at home. **Right** hardly dared to look into the store; but he would like to see if there was sold a few hands. He looked up at

the sign. Hand buy medicine written in large black letters. OTC drugs. It was not about buying hands. Boy, was he happy. You could probably not buy hands. You could probably not buy men and women either. What a relief. **Left** had also seen the sign.

- We've all been wondering about it, to no avail. He was almost angry that it was not hand-purchase. Still, he was happy. So they were certainly not purchased. He had heard something about adoption. That was when you could not have children. It adopted children who may not have parents. But purchased no. It might be bad. You could probably not. At the pharmacy, you could only buy pills and stuff. He tore Right's thumb and went shivering on.

The fishmonger's lorry

Just then an open truck filled with fish boxes moved quickly

around the corner behind them. They turned and saw the boxes on the truck bed, swinging dangerously. Water splashed over the edge of the boxes, and the twins jumped startled to side. The very moment the car went over a bump in the road, and two live eels fall down on the road just off the curb. A real live eel. Now he had seen it. **Right** was happy. Maybe it was some that the woman had dropped out of her pantyhose?

Well, no! He had just seen them jump out of the box on the car. Anyway! It could be that they were waiting for the woman hoping that they could be allowed to be in her pantyhose. They interested watched two eels disappearing down through a grate in the road.

- Did you see that brother? Eel!

Left had almost forgotten his brother in the bar arousal.

- Two eels, he corrected. **Right** had seen it; but he did not listen. He envisioned the woman with tights filled with eels. And how she could hardly walk. His brother's voice penetrated, and he nodded to answer.

They turned around in order to go on when they saw a man feeding some pigeons.

He bent down, bread lay on his palm, and the pigeons ventured right up and ate from his hand.

- He's got a hand to help him feed the pigeons.

Left was impressed.

- Yes, and they have the bread lying on the stomach. It's a strange thing to do!

Right had never lain down with food on his stomach. I wonder what my mother would say if he did something like that? Now, when he thought of his mother, he discovered how exhausted he really was. He would therefore like to go home.

- Do you know where we live?

Right moved close to her brother.

Left nodded.

- We'll be home soon. I know it all. About five minutes. He gently took her brother in the thumb, and they went on.

Reunion

- **Left**! **Right**! They could clearly hear their father's voice.
- I'm down here! They looked around, and no less than five feet in front of them, their father came running.
- Where on earth have you been? He scolded. All hile he shook them both greatly.
- Mom and I have been so scared. You've almost been away all day. The time is 4PM.

Was it really four?

Left had not noticed that it was getting late; but they had of course, been many places and seen so much. **Right** did not mind anything at all. He was just so happy to see his father. So never mind that it did a bit sore thumb, where his father still pressed him hard. Their father gave them a big hand pressure (hug), and they could see that he was crying. Was he really so sad to see them again? No, it had to be of joy. They had heard that you also cry when you were very happy.

They followed their father. Went through the door to the stairwell, and could hardly wait until they came up so much they had to tell their mother and father. When they came into the apartment gave their mother them a hand-pressure (hug) too, and she said nothing at all.

- You could also ....

Their father stopped in mid-sentence. There was no reason to talk about it. Now the boys were the safe at home.

- We have experienced so much, began **Left**.

- Yes, well, first off with the clothes, then you must have something to eat. You must be hungry and tired, exhorted their mother.

It was certainly true. They never thought that they had been so hungry before in their short lives.

They went to bed. With a "good night," they turned off the light and put both their heads on the pillow. Slumber was, after all, not the worst thing that existed.

Epilog:

The deaf people's world

As you probably know, there are many people, who can't hear anything. Some may even not hear or talk. The only way they can communicate are by typing or by using sign language. It is important that they are able to use their hands.

Sign language is a language where you use your hands and your facial expressions to say what you mean. When you speak, there are many words that can mean something very different. The word get a second opinion by changing the way you say it, and by the word put into a different context.
For example, the door: "There is a door in the living room." Or, "He dies tomorrow." Or the floor mat: "She was not allowed to go into town." Or, "We have a mat in front of our door." May mean in Danish either doormat or be allowed. As you can see, the deaf need to have different signs for the same word, just because the word can mean several things.
The deaf have both a deaf alphabet and signs that say a word. You can on the following pages both see the alphabet and some signs for common words that you use in everyday life.

Try to learn some of the characters. It might make you interested in learning the language and it would surely be good if you could also talk a bit with deaf people.

Ashtray / Haizara - ??

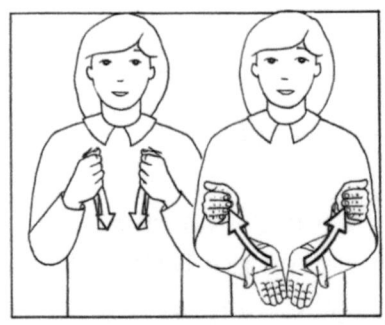

Bathtub / O furo - ???

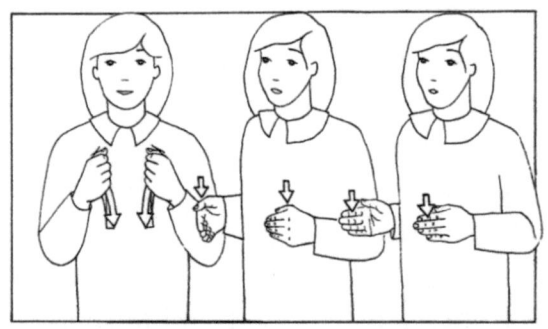

Bathroom / Basurumu - ?????

Picture / Gazo - ??

Turn signal / Uinka - ?????
Chime / Chaimu - ????

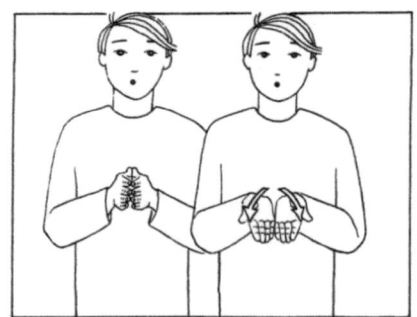

Book / Hon - ?
Magazine / Zasshi - Zasshi

Table
Teburu

Shower
Shawa

Cream
Kurimu

Ointment
Nanko

Chest freezer
Reitoko

Quilt
Kiruto

Door
Doa

Sweep
Suipu

Television
Terebi

Grandpa (dad's dad)
Ojichan

Grandma (dad's mom)
Sobo - O bachan

Cousin
Itoko

Good friends
Yoi tomodachi

Cousin
Itoko

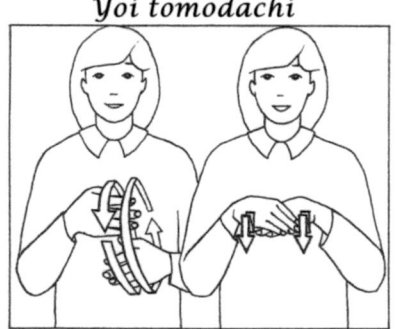

Playmate: Asobi nakama

Man - Otto

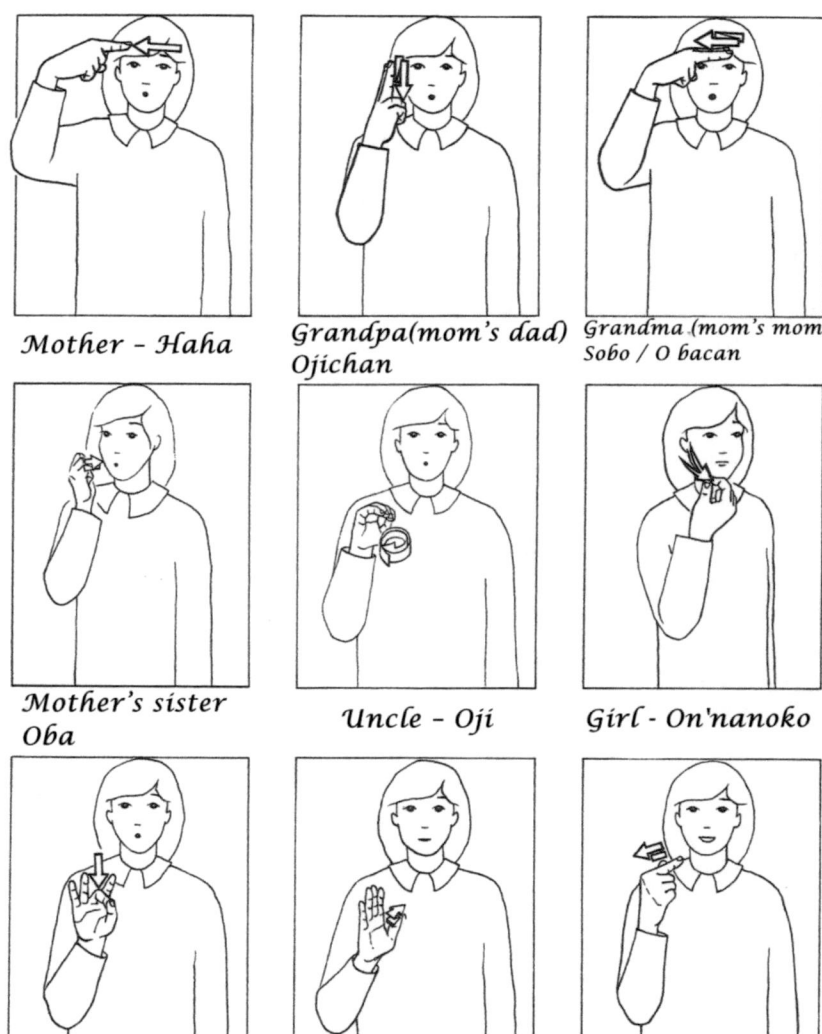

Mother – Haha

Grandpa(mom's dad)
Ojichan

Grandma (mom's mom)
Sobo / O bacan

Mother's sister
Oba

Uncle – Oji

Girl - On'nanoko

Son - Musuko

Sister - Shimai

Aunt - Oba

65

Baby - Akachan

Child - Kodomo

Grandparents
Sofubo

Brother - Ani

Woman- Josei

Daughter
Musume

Boy: Otokonoko

Family - Kazoku

Father - Chichi

Deaf international alphabet

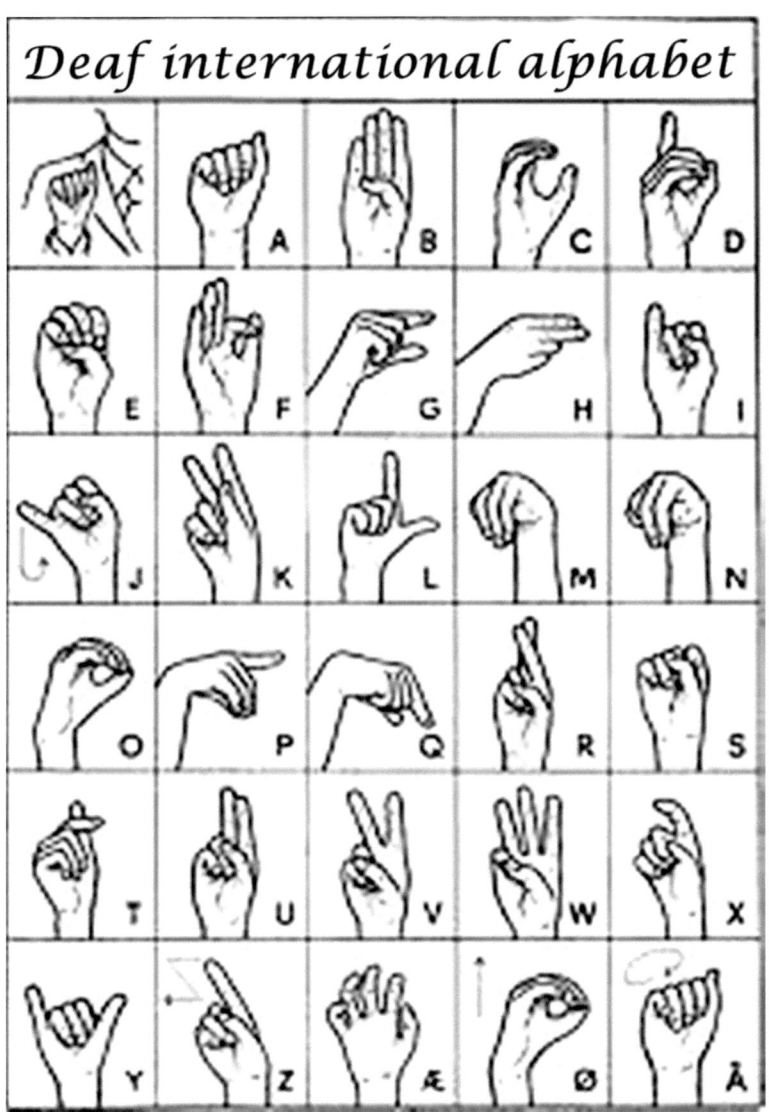